Kazumasa Ogawa

Costumes & customs in Japan

Kazumasa Ogawa

Costumes & customs in Japan

ISBN/EAN: 9783742840462

Manufactured in Europe, USA, Canada, Australia, Japa

Cover: Foto ©Andreas Hilbeck / pixelio.de

Manufactured and distributed by brebook publishing software
(www.brebook.com)

Kazumasa Ogawa

Costumes & customs in Japan

COSTUMES & CUSTOMS

IN

JAPAN.

BY

K. OGAWA,

PHOTOGRAPHER,

No. 1. Ichiwanshi Nichome, Kyabasu

TOKYO, JAPAN.

PHOTOTYPES, & FROM PHOTOGRAPHIC NEGATIVES
TAKEN BY HIM

Tea picking at Uji.

Old Court dress.

Costume, in former times,
of a daughter of the higher classes.

Hair-dressing.

Henry

Battle-dore and shuttle-cock play.

Koto playing.

The art of flower arrangement.

The ceremony of "Cha-no-yu."

Musical Entertainment.

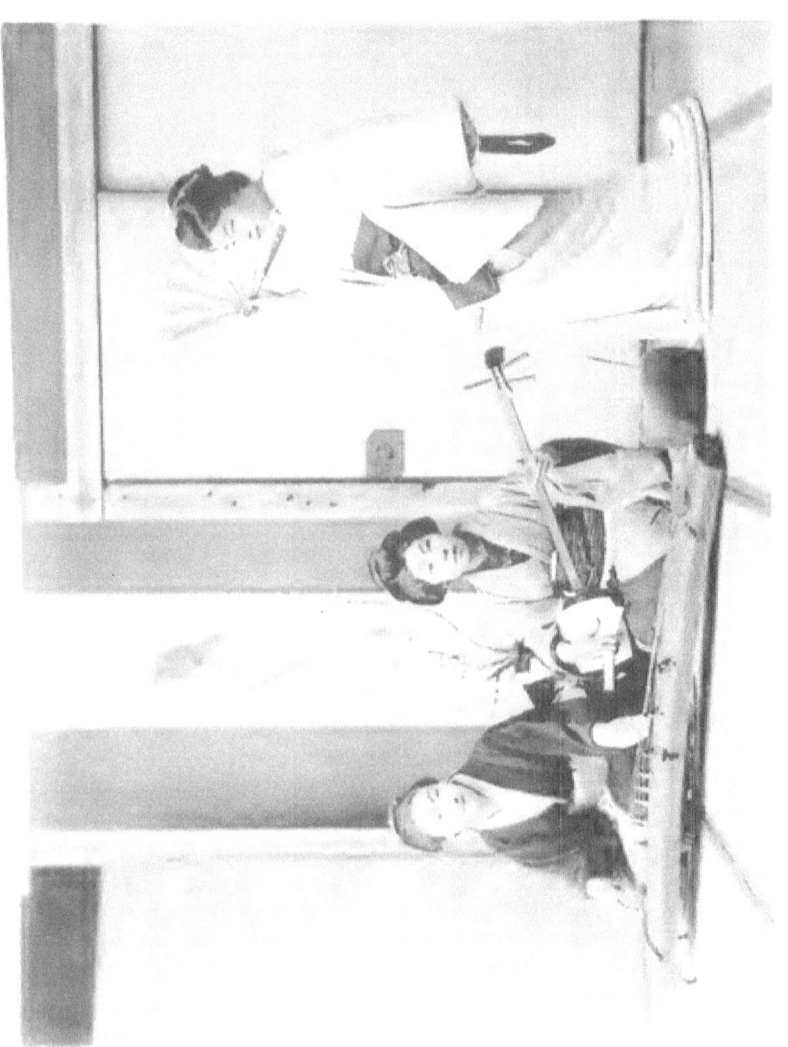

A Jinrikisha
ride to the flower shows.

Cotton-spinning.

Carpenters at work.

www.ingramcontent.com/pod-product-compliance
Lightning Source LLC
Chambersburg PA
CBHW022201020726
47496CB00008B/2820